written by **Harriet Ziefert**

Clara Ann Cookie, Go To Bed!

illustrated by **Emily Bolam**

HOUGHTON MIFFLIN COMPANY BOSTON 2000

Walter Lorraine Books

For Pam

Walter Lorraine (wr) Books

Text copyright © 2000 by Harriet Ziefert
Illustrations copyright © 2000 by Emily Bolam

Library of Congress Cataloging-in-Publication Data
Ziefert, Harriet.
  Clara Ann Cookie Go to Bed! / written by Harriet Ziefert:
Illustrated by Emily Bolam.
     p.   cm.
  Summary: After telling her mother that she does not want to
go to bed, Clara Ann Cookie has a problem getting her teddy
bear Popcorn to go to bed.
  ISBN 0-395-97381-3
  (1. Bedtime–fiction. 2. Teddy bears–fiction. 3. Toys–fiction.
4. Stories in rhyme.)
I. Bolam, Emily, ill. II. Title.
PZ8.3.Z47Cn   2000
[E]--dc21   99-25271
                                                      CIP

Printed in China for Harriet Ziefert, Inc.
HZI 10 9 8 7 6 5 4 3 2 1

When Clara Ann Cookie
Had to go to bed,
She stamped and she yelled
Till her face turned red.

Mother said, "To bed!"
Clara said, "No!"
Mother said, "Go!"
Clara said, "NO!"

Mother said, "Clara,
I'm leaving this room."
She shut Clara's door—
Her face full of gloom.

Clara then glared at
Her dolls and her bears.
"Now you go to sleep,
Or I'm going downstairs!"

All Clara's playmates
Climbed right into bed,
Except Popcorn, the teddy,
Who shook his big head.

"Now Popcorn," said Clara,
"Here's what I think.
I'll tell one more story,
I'll get one more drink."

Then Clara said, "To bed!"
Popcorn said, "No!"
Clara said, "Go!"
Popcorn said, "NO!"

Clara grabbed Popcorn.
She poked him quite hard.
"If you don't go to bed,
You'll be sent to the yard."

Said Clara to Popcorn,
"You needn't get mad.
You know perfectly well
You've been terribly BAD!"

"Have a two-minute time-out
And don't make a sound.
When you can act better,
Turn yourself around."

"There, there, little Popcorn,
I'm sorry I scolded.
You're looking so grumpy.
Your arms are all folded."

"I'll sing you a song.
I'll put you to bed.
Then I'll lie down beside you.
You'll be close to my head."

To sleep in a jiffy
Went Popcorn the bear,
And quick as a wink,
Before anyone knew—

Clara Ann Cookie
Was fast asleep, too!